Published in Great Britain in MMXXII by
Scribblers, an imprint of
The Salariya Book Company Ltd
25 Marlborough Place, Brighton BN1 1UB
www.salariya.com

ISBN: 978-1-913337-94-0

SALARIYA
SCRIBO BOOK HOUSE SCRIBBLERS

1 3 5 7 9 8 6 4 2

A CIP catalogue record for this book is available
from the British Library.

Editor: Nick Pierce

Visit
www.salariya.com
for our online catalogue and
free fun stuff.

PAPER FROM
SUSTAINABLE
FORESTS

THE SCRIBBLE MONSTERS!

SAY SORRY!

Guide to modern MANNERS

John Townsend

Carolyn Scrace

That's my favourite lorry!

I'll get it mended,
I really am so **sorry**.

We're the friendly Scribble Monsters,
We scribble lots of lines
And write how manners can be fun
On all our scribbly signs.

Sorry I made a mistake

Sorry I missed your birthday

Sorry if I was a pain –
I'll try not to be a pain again!

Some little children can forget
To leave kind words behind them...
We're here to scribble our advice
And find ways to remind them.

Think of others

Good manners show you care

Sorry about that!

Monsters with manners

Be polite

Pablo trips!

I am so **sorry**,
I must apologise.

He drops a jug of orange juice
On one of Inky's pies!

'**I**'m sorry' are two words that show
You'd like to put things right,
Because you care and feel regret...
And '**sorry**' is polite!

I'M SORRY!

BLOT
18 SCRIBBLE STREET
MONSTER TOWN
SM1 8SM

It can be fun to share our toys...
Oops, before those words are spoken,

Nibs has crashed poor Inky's lorry!

Oh dear, I think it's broken.

H.B.'s feeling really **sorry**
For getting in the way
And treading on poor Inky's foot...
So what should H.B. say?

I'm **sorry** for what I did just then.
Sorry I'm so jumpy,
It's just that I sat on a pin,
So now I'm feeling grumpy.

An elbow knocked a mug of tea,
Which splattered cold tea dregs.
Will anybody say they're **SORRY**
For splashing Inky's legs?

Someone's just gone to the kitchen,
To fetch another mug
And a cloth to make things cleaner...
Before a **'sorry hug'**.

Inky's had a day of upsets,
But at last it's all much better.
Blot has brought a drink of water...
Oops, now Inky's even wetter!

I'm **sorry** that I cried so loud,
I wish I hadn't shouted.

Not to worry, we're all still friends...
Our 'sorrys' can't be doubted!

It's bedtime and it's time to sleep,
So feeling warm and snug,
Someone wants to say **'I'm sorry'**
With one last **'sorry hug'**.

Now that feels a whole lot better,
Because a 'sorry' puts things right.
Nothing else is needed, only

I love you and goodnight.

Just say **sorry!**

Children who remember 'sorry'
When some things go wrong,
Get the Scribble Monsters singing
Their '**JUST SAY SORRY**' song!

Just say **sorry!**

Just say **sorry!**

H.B., Inky, Nibs and Pablo,
Blot and Smudge all sing
That when they hear you say **'I'm Sorry'**
It cheers up everything!

Just say **sorry!**

HAVE YOU HEARD THE MAGIC WORD?

Saying **SORRY** can make all the difference!

Well done for your MONSTER MANNERS

The Scribble Monsters wave goodbye
With friendly flags and banners
To help all children to remember
Those **SCRIBBLE MONSTER MANNERS!**

GOOD MANNERS ARE FREE!

CAN YOU HELP US FIND THE ANSWERS TO THIS QUIZ?

QUESTION 1

We give awards to children who say what two words?

I'M A SUPERSTAR SORRY

QUESTION 2

Children with good manners sparkle, when they say what?

QUESTION 3

When I accidentally trod on Inky's toe, should I have just said 'oops'?

QUESTION 4

When H.B. asks where my mop is, should I reply 'Bother, I forgot it'?

Look at the last page of the book to see if you are right!

MORE MONSTER QUESTIONS

QUESTION 5

I've broken Inky's lorry. Is it okay to just say 'I'll get it mended soon'?

QUESTION 6

What sort of hug should I give Inky?

QUESTION 7

Saying what always puts things right?

QUESTION 8

What is the name of the song we sing when children remember to say 'sorry'?

Look at the last page of the book to see if you are right!

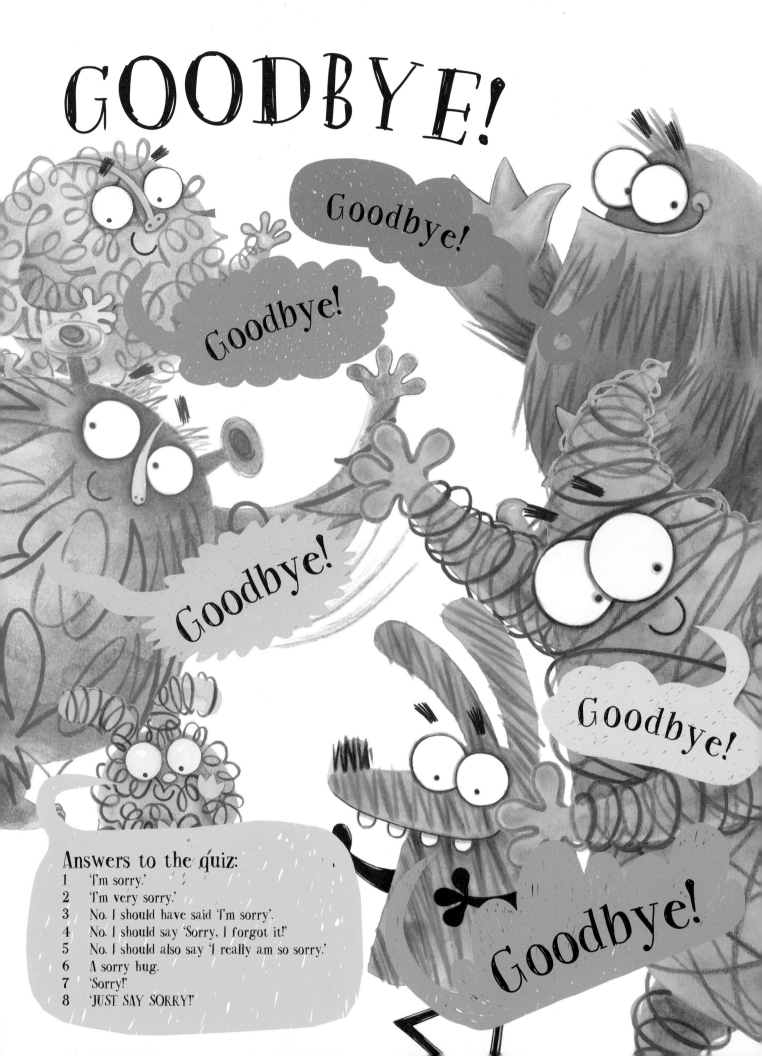

GOODBYE!

Answers to the quiz:
1 'I'm sorry.'
2 'I'm very sorry.'
3 No. I should have said 'I'm sorry'.
4 No. I should say 'Sorry, I forgot it!'
5 No. I should also say 'I really am so sorry.'
6 A sorry hug.
7 'Sorry!'
8 'JUST SAY SORRY!'